GRACE AND JOE

MARIBETH BOELTS
ILLUSTRATED BY MARTINE GOURBAULT

Albert Whitman & Company • Morton Grove, Illlinois

Text typeface: Weidemann Medium.
Typography: Karen Johnson Campbell.

Text © 1994 by Maribeth Boelts.
Illustrations © 1994 by Martine Gourbault.
Published in 1994 by Albert Whitman & Company,
6340 Oakton Street, Morton Grove, Illinois 60053.
Published simultaneously in Canada by
General Publishing, Limited, Toronto.
Printed in the United States of America.
10 9 8 7 6 5 4 3 2 1

Library of Congress Cataloging-in-Publication Data
Boelts, Maribeth, 1964—
Grace and Joe / by Maribeth Boelts; illustrated by Martine Gourbault.
p.   cm.
Summary: A preschooler finds a friend in her neighborhood mail carrier.
ISBN 0-8075-3019-0
[1. Friendship—Fiction. 2. Postal service—Letter carriers—Fiction.]
I. Gourbault, Martine, ill. II. Title.
PZ7.B635744Gr   1994   93-45920
[E]—dc20   CIP
                                                AC

To my childhood mail carrier friend, Wayne B. Cary. MB
For my friend Jennifer. MG

Once there was
a little girl
named Grace
who had three
big brothers,
three big sisters,
two cats
who ran away
from anyone
who tried to pet them,
and four goldfish
who stared at her
with black round eyes.

This little girl named Grace,
who lived in a house of people
and voices and music and noise,
was lonely, for she hadn't
yet found a friend.

There was Eddie next door,
but he always wanted to play
Good Guys and Bad Guys,
and Grace always had to be
a Bad Guy.

And there was Amy down
the street, but she played all
day with her suitcase of dolls
and doll clothes.

"The silver shoes go with the
silver dress," Amy would say.
"The black purse goes with the black jumpsuit."
Grace hated the tiny clothes with their tiny
snaps and the plastic shoes that got lost in the
thick summer grass. Her hands felt clumsy
and mad by the time she got one doll
ready to go to the dance.

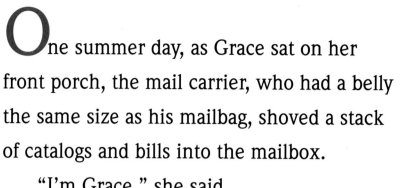

One summer day, as Grace sat on her front porch, the mail carrier, who had a belly the same size as his mailbag, shoved a stack of catalogs and bills into the mailbox.

"I'm Grace," she said. "What's your name?"

"I'm Joe," the mail carrier said, wiping the sweat from his face with a big red handkerchief. "You're the youngest in the family, aren't you?"

Grace nodded.

Joe lifted his bag over his shoulder and started slowly down the porch steps. "Well, it's nice to meet you."

Grace had an idea. She skipped into
the house and whispered in her mama's ear.

"I guess it would be okay, Grace," Mama
said. "Daddy and I have known Joe and his
family for a long time. But just go to the
houses on our street."

Grace followed Joe to each house,
talking and listening as they walked.

Grace learned that Joe had
two sons, but they were
grown and lived far away.
He had a dog named Raymond
who could balance a cookie
on the end of his nose. He liked
baseball and long letters
and books about real people.

They talked their way through
the hot days of summer,
and Joe learned that Grace
    liked to draw and paint
     and write stories with words
    only she could read.
He learned that she used to be
afraid of shadows, and that she
knew someone who had died.
Joe and Grace became friends,
and the summer passed.

It was soon fall, and everyone went back to school, except for Grace, who had one more year until she could go to kindergarten. She played in the quiet house and waited for Joe. Together they kicked their way through the heavy quilt of red, orange, and yellow leaves to deliver the mail.

Joe let Grace wear his rubber thumb stall,
and Grace held open the mailbox lids.

When winter came, Joe waited while Grace pulled on her snowsuit, mittens, boots, and hat. He never said, "Hurry up!" when the zipper stuck, or when she put her boots on the wrong feet. It was hard to talk through the wool scarf Grace's mother had tied over her mouth, and so, on the very cold days, the only sounds were the big steps and the little steps of two pairs of boots breaking through the icy crust of snow, and the clank of the metal mailbox lids.

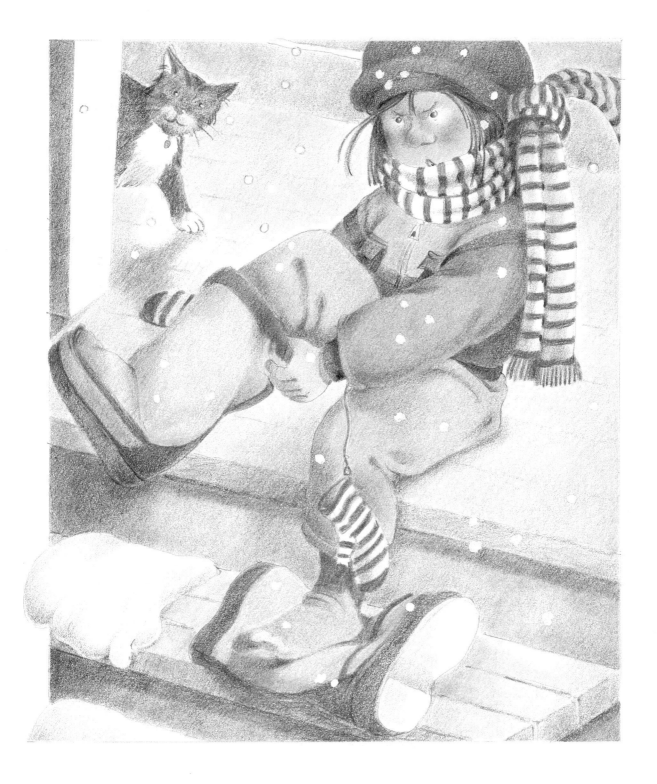

Once, when the snow fell all around them in soft, heavy flakes, Joe showed Grace how to make a snow angel. He lay down in the pillow of new snow and closed his eyes. Grace waited, thinking that he might decide to take a nap right there in her front yard. But at last he slowly moved his arms, then his legs, and then, carefully, carefully, he stood up.

Grace made an angel right next to Joe's, and the two angels stayed beautiful for one whole day.

It wasn't long before the snow changed to spring rain which left muddy brown puddles for Grace to jump over.

One day, there was a new mail carrier who moved fast.

"Where's Joe?" Grace asked from underneath her umbrella.

"He has a bad cold, but he told me to tell you he'll be back tomorrow," he said, stuffing the stack of mail into the neighbor's door before Grace had a chance to help.

"Oh," said Grace sadly, for Tomorrow seemed like a very long time from Today.

But the next day Joe was back, and he told Grace that he had seen a robin at his bird feeder, and Grace told Joe that the bulbs she had buried in the fall were turning into tulips.

When school was out for the summer, Grace's house filled up again with brothers playing drums in the basement, sisters talking on the telephone, and relatives visiting and laughing in the kitchen. Eddie popped wheelies on his bike, and Amy found a friend who had a suitcase full of dolls and doll clothes, too.

Grace played by herself, mostly, painting and drawing and writing letters that soon turned into words and words that turned into stories which she hung on her part of the wall in the bedroom.

One day Mama took her
shopping for new sneakers
and white socks and a
backpack, and she told Grace
that she would start
kindergarten very soon.

"I'll miss you," Joe said that afternoon on his route.

"You're my best friend," Grace said, as she squeezed his big hand tight.

They didn't say much after that. It would have been too sad.

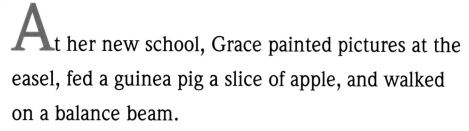

At her new school, Grace painted pictures at the easel, fed a guinea pig a slice of apple, and walked on a balance beam.

"Will you trace me if I trace you?" a girl named Sophia asked her at recess.

Sophia lay down on the warm concrete
and Grace traced her with a thick blue chalk.

"It's me!" Sophia said, clapping her hands.
"Now, let's trace you."

Grace lay still and squeezed her eyes shut
to keep out the bright September sun.

She felt Sophia's hand move over her head
and down her shoulder, and between her fingers.

"We're holding hands," Grace said,
looking at the two chalk girls on the
concrete. They reminded Grace of the angels that she and
Joe had made in the winter, and she told Sophia all about it
as they added fingernails and hair and laughing faces to
the chalk girls.

At home, Grace got out her good white paper and crayons,
and she wrote a story about a mail carrier, a little girl,
and a new friend named Sophia. But this time, she didn't
hang it up on her wall…

Joe hung it up on his.